Making Up Megaboy

by Virginia Walter

graphics by *Katrina Roeckelein*

Delacorte Press

Published by
Delacorte Press
a division of Random House, Inc.
1540 Broadway
New York, New York 10036

Making Up
Megaboy

To Richard Jackson, with thanks.
-V.W.

For my uncle
and Ethan.
-K.R.

Making Up Megaboy

Louise Jones

It was his birthday, three months ago today. He just turned thirteen. He was too old for a birthday party, but we gave him a fancy new mountain bike at breakfast. I thought he was pleased with it. He said he liked it.

I didn't think he even knew about my husband's gun. We never showed it to him. We never talked about it. I didn't think we needed a gun here in Santa Rosita; this is a safe place. But Robert wanted to be ready for anything. Robert kept the gun in the dresser, in his sock drawer. Robbie never had any reason to go in there.

Lord, I will never understand why he did it. I ask myself every day what went wrong, but I can't find any answers. He wasn't a bad boy. He didn't have bad friends, except maybe that Mexican boy who hung around for a while.

Why would Robbie shoot somebody on his birthday? It should have been a happy day.

REPORTER

Channel Two News is
live at the scene at the Main
Street Liquor Store in Santa Rosita.
An ambulance has just left with the
seriously wounded elderly man who has
operated this store for the past eight months.
He was shot at the store within the past two
hours. Police investigators say that a witness to
the incident saw a young boy shoot the victim, who has been identified as Jae Koh. The
boy got away on foot, leaving his bicycle outside the store. The police have no one in
custody at this time.
We'll keep on top of this story, Mark.
Back to you in the Channel
Two Newsroom.

I saw it happen. I was the only witness. I stopped in the liquor store to buy a six-pack on my way to my girlfriend's. I saw this little kid come riding up on his bike. He got off the bike real careful and locked it to the light pole. He had a big old blue backpack. He shrugged that backpack off his shoulders and just reached in and pulled out a gun, a .44, I think. I thought it was a joke or something. He said, "Mr. Koh?" I don't know if the old man even

VIETNAM VET

saw the gun. The boy looked like a silhouette against the open door. The man said "Yes?" like he wondered what the kid wanted. Then the boy shot him two or three times point blank and ran out of the store. I didn't see which way he went; I was trying to see if I could help the old guy, but there was too much blood. I was looking for a phone when the man from the barber shop came in.

I guess he heard the gunshots. He called the police and the ambulance. They took the old guy to the hospital, but he died the next day.

I never saw anything like it, a little kid about as big as a minute, just hauling off with a gun and shooting this guy in broad daylight right here in Santa Rosita. Man, he reminded me some of when I was in 'Nam. You'd see these itty-bitty Vietcong soldiers with guns nearly as big as they were. They could use 'em too.

BARBER

I heard the shots. I was just finishing up on Sam Cooper. I said, "Hold on there, Sam," and ran out to see what was going on. I saw this boy come running out of the liquor store like he was shot out of a cannon, and I went inside to look. At first I thought the big guy in there must have shot old Mr. Koh, but he said to call an ambulance.

I can't remember ever having a shooting on this street before. Raymond Lee used to have a lot of trouble with shoplifting. I guess that comes with the territory in a liquor store. You have to have eyes in the back of your head. It got to Ray after a while. I think that's why he retired when he did. Just couldn't take the aggravation from the kids.

I didn't know Mr. Koh very well. He took over the store less than a year ago. I'd go in and buy a soda in the afternoon most days. I'd say, "How's business?" He'd always say, "Could be better, could be worse." This is a pretty sleepy street now that the mall is open. The old-timers still like to come to me to get their hair cut though. They don't like going to those unisex places. They don't want some young girl putting mousse in their hair.

I was real sorry to hear that Mr. Koh didn't make it. I don't know when the store will open up for business again.

SANTA ROSITA TIMES

Boy, 13, Arrested In Liquor Store Shooting

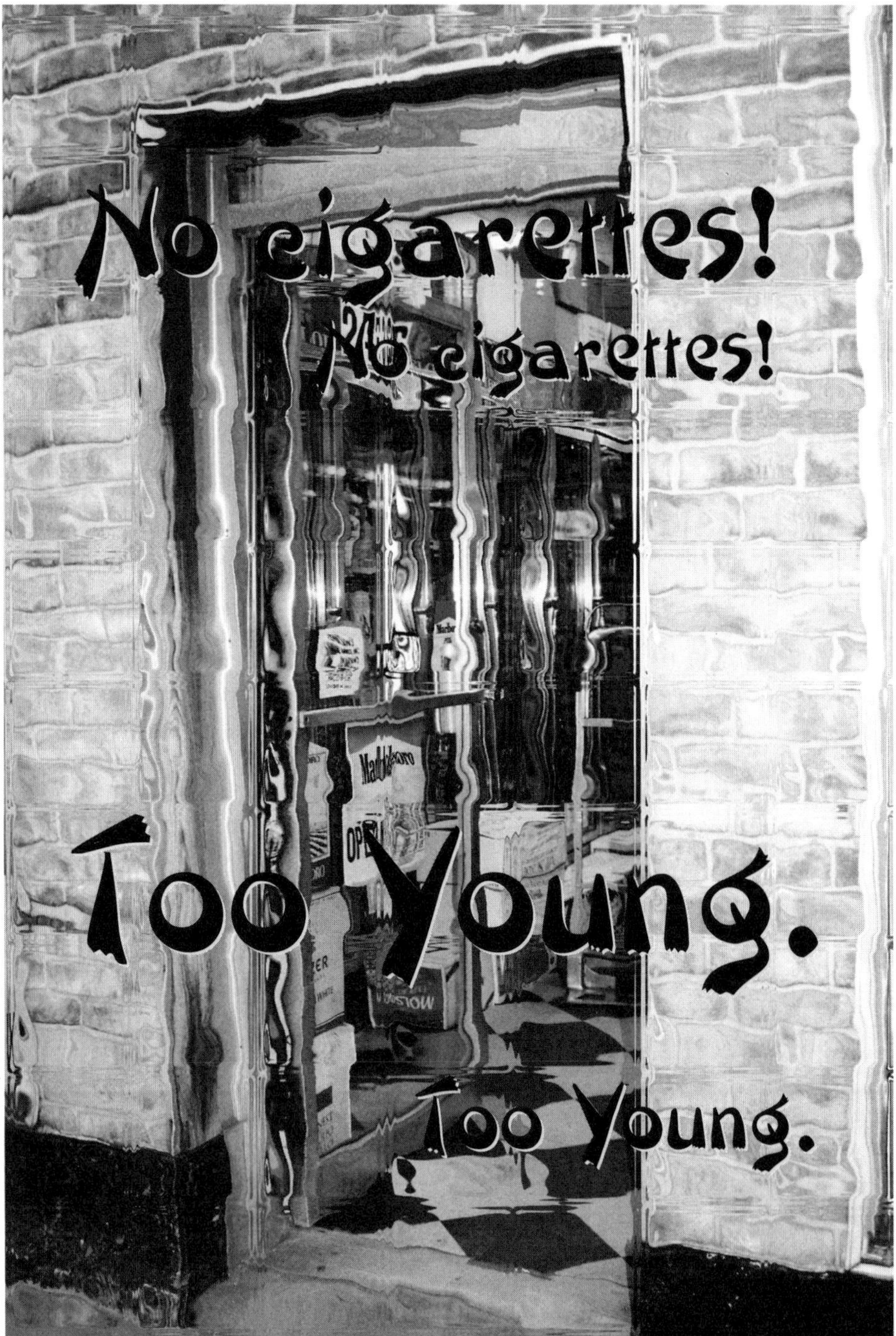
No cigarettes!
No cigarettes!
Too Young.
Too Young.

I used to go in that liquor store with Tiffany or my big sister. Angie used to buy cigarettes all the time from Mr. Lee. Then Mr. Koh, if that's his name, bought it, and he wouldn't sell cigarettes to kids. He was real mean about it. I went in there with Angie about a month ago, and she asked for a pack of Marlboros, and he just started yelling at us. "No cigarettes," he said. "No cigarettes! Too young. Not for nice girls. Too young." It really freaked me out. I told Tiffany about it, and we haven't gone back there since. It was a creepy, dark little store anyway.

Tara Jameson

Anchorman

The small town of Santa Rosita is reeling.
This suburb of Los Angeles is a quiet place, a quaint, old
fashioned town with nice homes and shady trees
and a Main Street that looks like it did in the 1950's.
People in Santa Rosita are in shock about the incident that
took place here two days ago, when a thirteen-year-old boy
shot and killed Jae Lin Koh, the elderly proprietor of a
liquor store on Main Street. The boy who allegedly
committed this violent crime has not
been identified officially because of his age, but
classmates at the Kennedy Middle School know who he
is, and they talked to Channel Two News reporter
Stacy Lynn. Stacy, what did the youngsters say?

Well, Mark, the students at Kennedy Middle School
are in shock. I talked to James Rowe, Tiffany Noguchi, and
Tara Jameson about the boy the police have in custody. They
described him as quiet, something of a loner, not somebody
who stood out in the crowd. He had a reputation for being a
good artist and having a vivid imagination. They were
unable to shed any light on a possible motivation for this
crime. There appears to be no obvious connection between
the victim and the boy.

Stacy, were you able to talk to the parents of the
boy?

No, Mark, they were not available for comment.
What about the victim's family, Stacy?
Mrs. Koh is in seclusion with her grown children,
Mark.

Good work, Stacy. Stay on top of that fascinating
story in Santa Rosita. Now for more on the rash of bank
robberies in the valley. Janet?

19

Ruben

Robbie liked to draw. He was good. He could draw tanks and planes that looked real, like in the newspaper. And he could make up space rockets and aliens and stuff too. Me and him made up stories all the time about a superhero called Megaboy. Megaboy is kind of like Popeye in those old comics, you know? He just looked ordinary until he ate his spinach, and then his muscles popped out all buff? Megaboy just looks all ordinary until he eats these special chips. I mean, they look just like regular potato chips or something, but they're really coated with megaspice that made him all strong and everything. Mostly Megaboy takes care of little kids that are in trouble and finds lost pets and stuff. We made up the stories together. Then Robbie'd draw the pictures, and I'd write out the words. Next summer we were going to turn Megaboy into a real strip, with the letters in bubbles coming out of people's mouths. I can't draw people like Robbie, but I can do the lettering real tough.

Robbie thought maybe he'd get a computer for his birthday, and then we could do all kinds of cool stuff.

Do you think they let him draw there up at juvie?

Correctional Officer

The subject, a thirteen-year-old white male, still shows no remorse for his action. He has unusually low affect. He is aware of his crime. He is able to recount his motions from the time he left school at three o'clock until he shot and killed an elderly Korean male at his place of business at 1435 Main Street at 4:45 pm. He claims that he is unable to remember anything after shooting Mr. Koh until he woke up in custody the following morning.

After two weeks, the subject still refuses to see his parents. He is being tutored by a staff teacher for four hours a day and sees the psychologist three times a week under the supervision of the court. As the youngest ward in the facility, he is kept separate from the older boys. He has shown little interest in recreational activities and spends most of his non-scheduled time sitting on his bunk and looking at the floor. The psychologist does not find that he is clinically depressed but rather in a state similar to that of post-traumatic shock victims. The subject has asked for drawing materials, and the psychologist advises that he be granted this request.

He wasn't in a gang or
anything. I mean, some of the guys
are real wannabes and wear the
baggy clothes and make hand signs
and act like they're all bad,
but Robbie was just a geeky little guy.
He wore regular clothes from
Sears or someplace. I think he kind
of liked my friend Tara. He was
always following us around. You'd be
walking down the hall or fooling
around on the lawn, and you'd look
back, and there he'd be. He gave Tara
this picture he drew of some
superhero carrying a girl in his arms,
and the girl looked just like Tara.
I didn't know he could draw so good.
Tara kept the picture,
but she never would have gone
with him or anything.
He was like, so immature.

Tiffany Noguchi

Yeah, he gave me
a picture he drew.

He said it was Megaboy
rescuing Taragirl from danger.

I said I wasn't in danger, and he said
you never know.

What a weirdo.

I taped the picture to the inside of my locker for a while;
it was fun to look at.

cop

We didn't find Robbie Jones until close to midnight. Of course, we didn't know his name yet; we didn't know who we were looking for. All we had to go on was the description from the witness and a blue backpack. There was nothing in the backpack except a scrap of paper that said "For Tara." We didn't know who Tara was either, not until later. We still don't know if there is a connection between Tara Jameson, Robbie Jones, and Jae Koh.

When we finally found the boy, he was up at Bowen Park, sitting in the crotch of a sycamore tree, holding the gun and shivering like crazy. We got a telephone tip that panned out; I figure it was from one of the dealers who use the park at night. We could see him right away; he wasn't hiding or anything. He didn't seem to see us or understand what we were saying or doing. We called to him to drop the gun, but he didn't respond. He didn't do anything, just shivered and held on to that gun. We didn't know if he had any bullets left, and we didn't know how he'd react to being apprehended. He looked like he was in shock. Finally I took a chance and got one of the officers to cover me while I approached him from the rear. I got up in the tree behind him, reached around, and just lifted the gun from his hand. Then he kind of toppled out of the tree. He got bruised and scratched up pretty good, but he didn't break any bones.

He was like a sleepwalker. We guided him to the black-and-white and took him down to juvenile hall. We knew he was the right kid, even if he wasn't talking. Later we got fingerprints and ballistics tests, and everything matched up. By the next day, he was talking anyway. He said he killed the old man. He just never did say why.

ROBERT JONES

Robbie wasn't interested in girls. He never talked about this Tara or any other girl. I wish he had; that would have been more normal. Hell, when I was his age, I was already making out with girls and thinking about doing a lot more things. Robbie was a little backward that way, and I'm afraid he was kind of a sissy. I could never get him interested in sports. I'd give him sports equipment and take him to team tryouts, but he never had the drive to keep it up. He was pretty small for his age; maybe that's why. A late bloomer, my wife called him.

Ruben

Robbie's dad had a gun. Robbie showed it to me one time when I was over at his house. It wasn't a hunting rifle, like my uncle's. It was a small gun, a handgun, I think you call it. It was hidden in the back of a drawer with his socks. It made me feel scared to look at it, and I didn't like being in his parents' room, even if they weren't home. Man, I thought we were going to get caught for sure. Robbie said he took it out and held it sometimes. He said it felt cold and heavy. I touched it, and he was right.

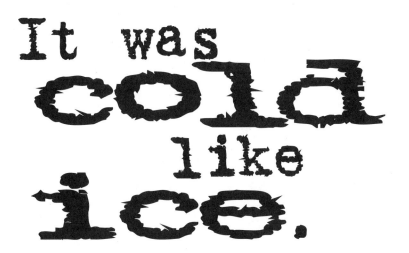

It was cold like ice.

TEACHER

He wasn't an A student, but he wasn't at the bottom of the class either. He did his homework on time and came to class regularly. He was one of the better math students. He liked doing word problems. That's the only time he would volunteer an answer, when we did word problems. Sometimes his attention wandered, and I would have to remind him to stop daydreaming. But a lot of children are daydreamers at this age; it's hormones, you know. At least he wasn't disruptive like some of the boys.

He was never a behavior problem. He wasn't one of the popular crowd, but he seemed to get along all right with his classmates. At least he didn't get into fights. I certainly didn't think of him as a violent child.

I still can't believe it. How could a quiet, ordinary seventh-grade boy just take out a gun and shoot somebody?

Tara
Jameson

We got on the news. That blond reporter from the Channel Two News came and talked to us after school. Everybody was talking about Robbie Jones and what he did. She asked us if we knew him and what he was like. We told her lots of stuff about how he was always following me around and how he was always drawing space creatures and superheroes. We looked pretty good when it came on. They had us stand behind the reporter on the school lawn while she was talking into the camera. We looked all serious, except Tiffany kept giggling. I don't know what James was doing there. He just came crowding in, acting all big. He's real cute though.

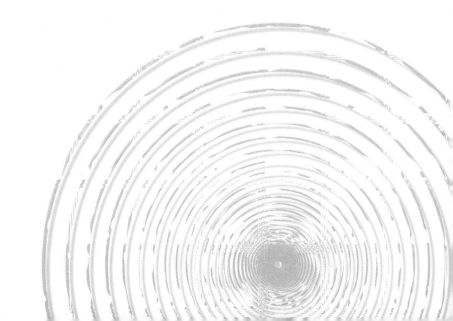

Mrs. Koh

I do not know this boy who shot my husband.
I never saw him in the store.
What kind of boy shoots an old man who was always kind to children?
What kind of boy is this?
In our country, in Korea, children respect old people.
Children do not have guns in Korea.
What kind of country is this?

Ruben

I guess I was his best friend since he moved here in fourth grade. We both liked comics a lot. We started making up Megaboy last year. We came to my house to draw because his mom and dad are kind of strict and they don't like me too much. He told his mom he was going to the library to study all the time, but he really came over to my place. I don't think they like Mexicans very much at his house. Robbie didn't care though. Sometimes he made Megaboy look Mexican and sometimes he looked white like him. Megaboy's real parents are from another planet, but he had to come to Planet Earth when a comet destroyed his family's city. His parents saw it coming and put him in a rocket with lots of Earth money and a lifetime supply of megachips so he could survive here. He lives in a regular house, and people think his parents are there, but he really lives alone. All his megachips are locked in an underground storage vault that he made. He just keeps enough in the house for emergencies. And he's always got some in his backpack when he goes out of the house. He has to go to school so nobody will suspect he's really Megaboy. His earth name is Frankie Montalban. See, he could be Mexican, huh? It's not the same making up Megaboy without Robbie to draw the pictures.

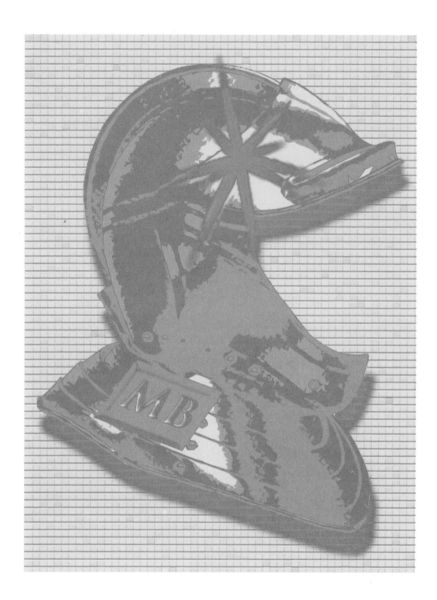

Classmate

I sat next to him in social studies.
He was always doodling on his paper instead of paying attention.
He drew pictures of spaceships mostly. He didn't talk much except
to his friend Ruben. I never thought about Robbie Jones at all
until I heard that he'd shot Mr. Koh. Then I thought about him
all the time and wondered what he was really like inside. He
looked so ordinary on the outside, just a boy you'd never
think twice about. You would never know that inside that
skinny body in a polo shirt and jeans was a person planning
to kill somebody. It makes me look differently at
everybody now. How can you tell what anybody is
really like?

Some of the girls were crying in school the
next day, but I don't think they were really sad.
It's not like they cared about Mr. Koh. Some of
the kids were excited because our school was on the
news. They even interviewed Tiffany and Tara and James,
and they got on the news too. It was kind of silly; those kids
didn't know him any better than I did, and now they
are famous too.

Principal

Our school doesn't deserve this kind of publicity. This is a good community. We believe in family values. Our children don't get into this kind of trouble. Why didn't they do a story about our basketball team or the talent show? Now when people think about Kennedy Middle School, they will associate us with a senseless killing.

At least the Jones boy didn't commit his crime on the school campus. Thank heavens for small favors. I have asked the PTA to address this issue in its programming over the coming year. We need to rebuild our good image. Robbie Jones is not typical of the children in this community.

Mrs. Koh

Nobody cared about my husband.
On the news and in the paper they all wanted to talk about
this little boy with a gun.
What a terrible thing it is, for a young boy to have a gun.
What a terrible thing it is, for a young boy to shoot someone.
But did they ever talk about the man he shot?
Jae Lin Koh was a good man who came to this country to work hard
and raise his family well.
What do they know about him?
Do they know that he liked to watch American baseball when
the Dodgers were playing?
Do they know that his favorite meal was hot dogs with kimchi?
Do they know that he played the accordion for his grandchildren?
Do they think his life did not matter because he was old and Korean?
What do they know about him and about me?
Do they know how much I miss him?
I do not know if I can stay in this country.
Will I see my grandson take a gun and shoot some other old man?

고 재인

1928 - 1998

RUBEN'S MOTHER

He was a nice boy, so quiet and polite. When he came to see my Ruben, he always said hello and please and thank you. He was nice to the babies; he didn't tease them like some of the big boys do. Robbie and Ruben didn't do rowdy things. They just sat at the kitchen table and read comics and drew pictures. I can't believe he did that terrible thing. He was not a boy who would kill. It hurts my Ruben to think about it, his friend doing something like that. I know he misses him. It is confusing for him because he feels bad about Mr. Koh too. I never knew Robbie's family. He does not live in our neighborhood, although the boys attended the same school. His mother must be very sad.

Reverend Lewis

I pray for Mr. and Mrs. Jones and for their son, Robbie, continually. This trial is testing the parents' faith in God. Robbie has been baptized, and he is under the protection of the Church. I do not know why the Devil chose this boy to tempt or why Robbie turned away from the teaching of this Church as he did. I can only hope that he will repent and be forgiven.

Louise Jones

We went to church together as a family, not every Sunday but pretty often. It's not like we didn't teach him right from wrong. "Thou Shalt Not Kill." I'm sure they taught him the Ten Commandments in Sunday school. I might have been too easy on him, but Robert was very strict.

Robbie played with toy guns when he was little, of course, just cops and robbers or cowboys and Indians or whatever games the neighborhood boys played. It was just a game, kid stuff. Robert always wanted him to get out and play with other boys; he thought his son spent too much time by himself in his room, reading and drawing. Sissy stuff, Robert called it.

He never did show his emotions much, except that one time when his dog ran away. Robbie cried and cried, as though his heart was broken. Robert said he'd buy him a new dog, but Robbie wouldn't hear of it.

Reverend Lewis says I shouldn't blame myself. I tried to be a good mother to that boy. I never worked after he was born. I was almost always home after school. When he was little, I would read him Bible stories and fairy tales and make him pancakes in shapes like bears and elephants. It was easier to make him happy then.

Two cops came to talk to me at
school a couple of days after it happened.
They asked me if Robbie and I were friends.

Right. Like I'd really be friends with someone
like Robbie Jones.

They asked me if I knew why Robbie'd have my name
on a paper in his backpack. I said maybe he liked me.
Tiffany thought so, and he did give me that drawing.

I didn't tell the cops about the Megaboy-Taragirl picture
though. Now that Robbie is famous,
that picture might be valuable.
Maybe I can sell it to the *Enquirer* or something.
I wish he'd signed it. His autograph would probably
be worth a lot.

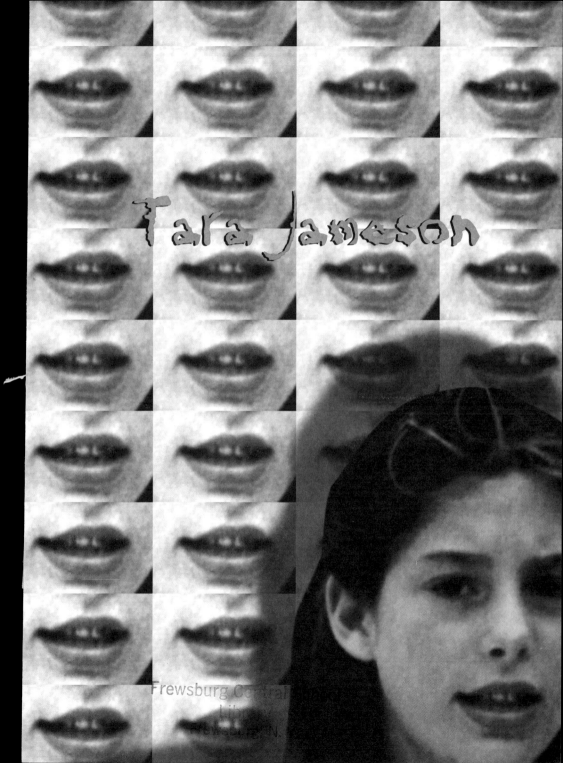

Tara Jameson

Ruben

Robbie liked Tara a lot. He thought she was really pretty. He tried to draw her sometimes and put her in the Megaboy pictures. He used to try to get me to go with him to follow her when she was with her friends or her big sister. It made me feel stupid, so I didn't do it. Tara Jameson is kind of wild. She doesn't get in trouble though, because her parents have money. Robbie thought she was lonely. I don't know why he thought that; she was always with a bunch of kids. I don't know if Robbie ever said anything to her. He was shy about talking, even to me. Mostly he just drew pictures.

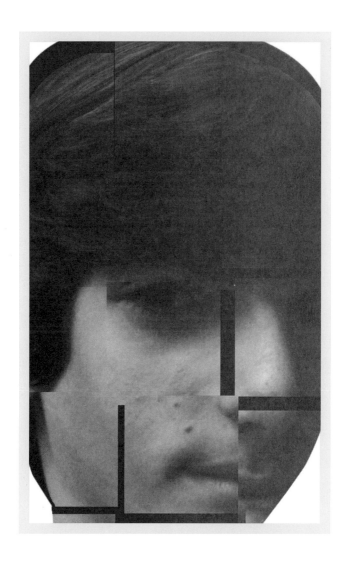

Correctional Officer

The subject is still withdrawn. He does not initiate conversation with any staff members except to ask for drawing materials. He draws for at least an hour a day. His pictures appear to depict a superhero whom he calls Megaboy. Many drawings feature a young female whom he calls Taragirl. The psychologist speculates that Megaboy is a metaphor for the person Robbie Jones would like to be, an alternative persona, so to speak.

ATTORNEY

Mr. Jones does not realize the seriousness of Robbie's situation. His son committed a capital crime, a felony, to which there was a witness and to which he has confessed. There are no facts in dispute about his actions. It is just fortunate that he hadn't turned fourteen; I don't think I could have prevented his being tried as an adult if he had been a year older. I think I might have been more effective in securing an alternative treatment facility for Robbie if his father had been cooperative with the social workers and probation officers who were investigating his case. We were unable to establish any kind of motive for the crime. To this day, I don't know why Robbie Jones killed Jae Lin Koh. I wonder if Robbie even knows why he did it. He'll have a lot of time to think about it. He won't be released until he is twenty-five.

Robbie Jones

"The First Earth Adventure of Megaboy"

Frankie Montalban climbed to the highest branch of the tallest tree in the park at the top of the hill. He opened a packet of megachips and ate them. Instantly, his eyes began to glow with special intelligence and his muscles bulged with special strength. Frankie Montalban was now the superhero Megaboy. Megaboy reached into his backpack for the special signaling device. He set the dial to the usual channel, Home.

Megaboy performed the familiar ritual even though he did not expect to receive an answer. He knew that his parents would bring him home when it was safe for him to return. Until that time, he would continue to send the signal every week. His faith was strong.

Something was different this time. Megaboy felt a vibration through the entire tree after he sent his signal into deep space. His signaling device began to pulse, and he received the answer he had been waiting for for so long. His parents were coming to get him. The spaceship would touch down in exactly one hour. His parents must have been waiting for his signal. Megaboy's heart swelled with joy.

But what was this? Another signal was coming in from nearby, interfering with the signal from deep space. A human child was in trouble. Megaboy could not ignore the call. The signal was very intense. He followed the signal to a large compound on the outside of town. This fenced installation was the juvenile correctional facility for young Earthlings who committed crimes and needed punishment.

The signal was emanating from a human boy locked in a room deep inside the facility. He was not crying, but his soul was in great pain. Megaboy knew that this was not really a bad child. This was just a human child born on the wrong planet. Megaboy did not hesitate. He quickly leaped over the barbed-wire fence. He moved from shadow to shadow until he was standing outside the human child's window. He used his megamindpower to loosen the window from its frame and silently slipped inside.

"I knew you would come, Megaboy," said the human child.

Megaboy took a packet of megachips from his pouch and gave it to the child. The boy slowly opened the package and ate every chip. His eyes began to glow, and his muscles began to bulge. Together Megaboy and the human child escaped from the cold, lonely room, vaulted the fence, and raced to the park. There was a scorched triangle of grass where the spaceship had landed and taken off again.

Megaboy looked sad for a minute, and the child asked him what was wrong.

"It is nothing, human child," he said. "They will return. You may wait with me, and we will work together to defeat the forces of evil who oppress children on this planet. You have a debt to pay to your society, and I feel that I have important work to do here. Someday we will go home."

Soon children in trouble everywhere on Earth knew that Megaboy and his companion, Humanchild, would hear their unspoken cries for help and come to rescue them from danger and anguish.

Ruben

I think I know why he went to Bowen Park after he killed Mr. Koh. We used to pretend that Megaboy went there to signal to his parents. He wanted them to know that he was all right. Megaboy had a special signaling device that he would use. They never answered, but he believed that they got his signals. Megaboy believed that someday his planet would be restored, and his parents would send for him to go back there.

I don't think Robbie was trying to call his parents though. He was probably scared to death. His old man would whip him, and his mom would cry for sure. I don't know which was worse. Maybe he was trying to call Megaboy.

ROBERT JONES

WHAT WAS HE TRYING TO PROVE ANYWAY? IT WAS HIS BIRTHDAY. HE HAD A BRAND-NEW EXPENSIVE MOUNTAIN BIKE. WE GAVE HIM ANYTHING HE WANTED, WITHIN REASON. WE LOVED HIM, FOR CHRIST'S SAKE. HELL, WE STILL LOVE HIM. HE'S STILL OUR SON, EVEN IF HE IS A MURDERER.

I THINK IT MUST HAVE BEEN A DARE OR SOMETHING. SOMEBODY DARED HIM TO DO IT, AND HE JUST DIDN'T THINK WHAT HE WAS DOING. MAYBE IT WAS THAT MEXICAN KID HE USED TO HANG AROUND WITH UNTIL I SET HIM STRAIGHT. I KNEW HE WAS A BAD INFLUENCE. OR MAYBE THE OLD GUY PROVOKED HIM SOMEHOW. I WISH ROBBIE WOULD JUST TELL SOMEBODY WHY HE DID IT.

THE LAST TIME I SAW ROBBIE WAS AT THE COURT HEARING. HE LOOKED SO LITTLE, STANDING NEXT TO HIS LAWYER. I GOT HIM THE BEST LAWYER I COULD FIND, A LOT OF GOOD THAT DID. SIX THOUSAND DOLLARS DOWN THE DRAIN, RIGHT THERE.

THEY TELL MY WIFE AND ME WE CAN'T VISIT ROBBIE OUT THERE AT THE JUVENILE HALL UNTIL THE SHRINK SAYS IT'S OKAY. THAT DOESN'T SEEM RIGHT. HE'S OUR SON. LOUISE CRIES ALL THE TIME. SHE DOESN'T LIKE TO LEAVE THE HOUSE. SHE SAYS PEOPLE LOOK AT HER FUNNY. I THINK SHE'D FEEL BETTER IF SHE COULD SEE HIM. I DON'T KNOW WHAT WE COULD SAY TO HIM THOUGH.